When Small Is Tall

AND OTHER READ-TOGETHER TALES

A Random House PICTUREBACK®

When Small Is Tall

AND OTHER READ-TOGETHER TALES

Prepared by the Bank Street College of Education

Written by Seymour V. Reit
William H. Hooks
Betty D. Boegehold

Illustrated by Lynn Munsinger

RANDOM HOUSE 🏠 New York

Text copyright © 1985 by Bank Street College of Education. Illustrations
copyright © 1985 by Lynn Munsinger. All rights reserved under International
and Pan-American Copyright Conventions. Published in the United States
by Random House, Inc., New York, and simultaneously in Canada by
Random House of Canada Limited, Toronto.

Library of Congress Cataloging in Publication Data: Main entry under title: When
small is tall. Stories based on Aesop's fables. Contents: When small is tall/
retold by Seymour V. Reit—Tiny Tortoise and Harry the Hare/retold by
William H. Hooks—Little Red Ant and Plump White Dove/retold by Betty
D. Boegehold. SUMMARY: Three of Aesop's fables are retold with rebuses and
repeatable refrains. 1. Fables. 2. Rebuses. [1. Fables. 2. Rebuses]
I. Munsinger, Lynn, ill. II. Reit, Seymour. When small is tall. III. Hooks,
William H. Tiny Tortoise and Harry the Hare. IV. Boegehold, Betty
Virginia Doyle. Little Red Ant and Plump White Dove. V. Aesop's fables.
PZ8.2.W48 1984 398.2′452 [E] 83-9811 ISBN: 0-394-85836-0
(trade); 0-394-95836-5 (lib. bdg.)

Manufactured in the United States of America   1 2 3 4 5 6 7 8 9 0

To Parents

This book, based on tales from Aesop, is designed for you and a young child to read together. Pictured animals and objects appear throughout the stories in place of words, and your child can participate right away in "reading" these rebuses as you read the printed words aloud.

While you read the story, move your finger under the words you are saying. This will help your child understand that we read each line from left to right and the page from top to bottom. The child will also begin to see that the little black squiggles called letters represent "talk written down." Such learning is new to the young child and basic to his or her later reading success.

Each story has a refrain that is easy to recognize and remember. Once the child is familiar with the book, encourage him or her to say the refrains in the balloons. Then let the child try telling you the whole story in his or her own words.

Sharing a book in a warm and satisfying way is an inviting introduction to the joys of reading. As the process provides a sense of accomplishment, the child's pride and self-confidence will be reinforced by the theme running through these stories—"Power to the small!"

—Seymour V. Reit,
William H. Hooks,
Betty D. Boegehold

THE BANK STREET COLLEGE OF EDUCATION

WHEN SMALL IS TALL

Small Mouse was the smallest animal
in the whole jungle. But all day
she went around singing:

Maybe I'm small,
But I act TALL!

The other jungle animals teased Small Mouse
when she sang her song.

The  in the trees
laughed at her.

The  in the river
laughed at her.

The  in the field
laughed at her.

The  in his cave
laughed at her.

"You're the smallest of us all!" they shouted.
But Small Mouse just went on singing her song:

Maybe I'm small,
But I act TALL!

When King Lion heard Small Mouse's song, he laughed the loudest of them all.

King Lion laughed so loud, he had a coughing fit. He had to hold his paws up in the air while the  pounded on his back.

But Small Mouse went right on singing:

Maybe I'm small,
But I act TALL!

One day King Lion walked under a tall

SNAP!

He stepped right into a trap.

"HELP! Get me out of here!" roared King Lion.

The jungle animals ran back and forth,
fussing and shouting.

The  didn't know what to do.

The  didn't know what to do.

The 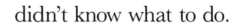 didn't know what to do.

And neither did the
Then Small Mouse came along singing:

Maybe I'm small,
But I act TALL!

"I will set King Lion free," she said.

The animals all looked at Small Mouse
and shook their heads.

"You're too small," said the

"You're too small," said the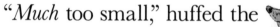

"You're too small," said the

"*Much* too small," huffed the

But Small Mouse went on singing:

Maybe I'm small,
But I act TALL!

Then she scurried over to the tall
and began to chew and gnaw the ropes.

Small Mouse gnawed through one strand of
rope. She gnawed through another. Then another.
Soon she had gnawed a big hole in the net—
big enough for the lion to wiggle through!

King Lion jumped to the ground, free at last.

The lion picked up the mouse in his big furry paw.

He said in a loud voice:

MAYBE SHE'S SMALL,
BUT SHE SURE ACTS <u>TALL</u>!

The jungle animals all cheered, "Hurray for
Small Mouse! Hurray! Hurray!"

Tall-Small Mouse was pleased. She smiled and
said, "I knew it all the time."

TINY TORTOISE AND HARRY THE HARE

Once there was a big, flibberty-jibberty rabbit named Harry the Hare.

He was always bragging:

I'm Harry the Hare,
And no one will dare
To race with me!

Harry called to Miss Squirrel,

he shouted to Mr. Fox,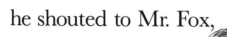

and he yelled at Mrs. Bear:

"WHO WILL RACE WITH ME?"

"Not me!" chirped Miss

"Never!" barked Mr.

"Not today," growled Mrs.

So with a hop-skip-hop, Harry bounced along,
still bragging:

I'm Harry the Hare,
And no one will dare
To race with me!

Suddenly Harry stopped, right in the middle of a hop and a skip.

Somebody was calling to him.

"Where are you?" cried Harry the Hare, looking all around.

"I'm right down here," said a very small voice.
"I'm Tiny Tortoise."

Harry looked down and laughed. He said to
Tiny Tortoise:

I'm Harry the Hare,
And no one will dare
To race with me!

"I will!" said Tiny Tortoise bravely.

When the other animals heard him, they all hurried over.

"How long will the race be?" asked Miss

"From here to the pond, and back!" cried Mr.

"How can you ever hope to win?"

whispered Mrs.  to Tiny Tortoise.

Tiny Tortoise smiled and whispered back:

I can do it,
If I stick to it!

"Ready! Get set! GO!" cried Mr.

With a fast hop-skip-hop, Harry the Hare was
soon out of sight. Tiny Tortoise crawled slowly
along on his stubby little legs.

Soon Harry the Hare reached the pond. Then he laughed
and said, "Tiny Tortoise is so slow. I'll have time
for a nap, and I can still win the race."

Tiny Tortoise crawled along and crawled along. He passed some sweet grass that he wanted to nibble. But he kept on crawling.

He said to himself:

I can do it,
If I stick to it!

Soon he reached the pond where Harry the Hare was sleeping. Tiny Tortoise wanted to drink some water. But he kept on crawling.

He said to himself:

I can do it,
If I stick to it!

Up ahead, Tiny Tortoise could see Miss
Mr. 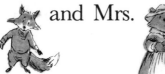 and Mrs.

He wanted to stop and rest. But he kept on crawling.
Again he said to himself:

I can do it,
If I stick to it!

Harry the Hare woke up at last. With a quick
hop-skip-hop, he started running once more. Then he
spied Tiny Tortoise, almost at the finish line!

Harry the Hare raced as fast as he could go.
But Tiny Tortoise crossed the finish line first!

"Hip!" cried Miss

"Hip!" cheered Mr.

"HURRAY!" yelled Mrs.

"Tiny Tortoise won the race!" they all shouted.
"How," asked Harry the Hare, "could a Tiny Tortoise
ever beat <u>me</u>?"
Tiny Tortoise just smiled and said:

I KNEW I COULD DO IT,
IF I STUCK TO IT!

LITTLE RED ANT AND PLUMP WHITE DOVE

Little Red Ant and Plump White Dove were
talking one day. Little Red Ant said:

Let's be friends,
Good and true.
You help me
And I'll help you.

Plump White Dove laughed and said softly:

Coo, coo.
I just can't see
How a little red ant
Can ever help me!

Suddenly a fierce gust of wind blew Red Ant
into the brook.

She called out to White Dove, "Help! Help!
Save me!"

White Dove flew down quickly. Gently, he lifted
Red Ant out of the water. Then he set her on a
big gray ⬤ in the green 🌾

Little Red Ant looked up at Plump White
Dove and said:

> You're a friend,
> Good and true.
> You helped me,
> Now I'll help you.

Plump White Dove laughed again and said:

> Coo, coo.
> I just can't see
> How a little red ant
> Can ever help me!

Little Red Ant answered, "Wait and see."

White Dove perched high in the
and began to clean his feathers.

But danger was coming!

The plump dove didn't see the Hunter with
his  and  who was hiding
behind a big  !

The Hunter watched the bird. Quiet as a

sly as a he crouched

behind the

Smiling, the Hunter said to himself:

> Soft, plump Dove,
> Fat and white,
> I'll have you
> For supper tonight!

Little Red Ant began to crawl toward the Hunter.
She raced

across the gray

through the green

under a yellow

over a brown

and
right
up the
Hunter's
leg.

Then she bit his leg very HARD!
"Yeeeoow! Ouch!" yelled the Hunter.

He dropped his  and
and began hopping up and down.

Whirrr! Whirrr!

Away flew Plump White Dove, high into the blue sky, where he was safe.

Little Red Ant crawled back

over the brown

under the yellow

through the green

to the big gray

Sitting on the big  Red Ant
waved to White Dove.

High in the sky above her, White Dove
looped and swooped happily.

Then he called:

COO, COO.
NOW I SEE
HOW A LITTLE RED ANT
<u>CAN</u> HELP ME!